Play, Mozart, Play!

Peter Sís

Greenwillow Books
An Imprint of HarperCollinsPublishers

Play, Mozart, Play!

Copyright © 2006 by Peter Sís

All rights reserved. Printed in the United States of America.

www.harpercollinschildrens.com

Black line and watercolors were used to prepare the full-color art.

The text type is 28-point Lapidary333 BT.

Library of Congress Cataloging-in-Publication Data

Sís, Peter, (date).

Play, Mozart, play! / Peter Sís.

  p. cm.

"Greenwillow Books."

ISBN-10: 0-06-112181-9 (trade bdg.) ISBN-13: 978-0-06-112181-4 (trade bdg.)

ISBN-10: 0-06-112182-7 (lib. bdg.) ISBN-13: 978-0-06-112182-1 (lib. bdg.)

1. Mozart, Wolfgang Amadeus, 1756-1791—Juvenile literature.

2. Composers—Austria—Biography—Juvenile literature. I. Title.

ML3930.M9S57 2006 780.92—dc22 2005030152

First Edition 10 9 8 7 6 5 4 3 2 1

Greenwillow Books

To Milos Forman

Wolfgang Amadeus Mozart

was a famous composer

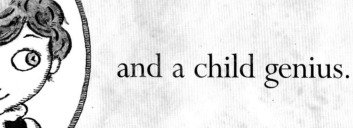

and a child genius.

His father
turned him
into a child sensation!

LONDON

AMSTERDAM

Mozart played in London
and Amsterdam
and Paris,

PARIS

MUNICH

VIENNA

SALZBURG ~ Home

ROME

and in Munich
and Vienna
and Rome.

Mozart played for kings and princes and dukes

Court of King George III ~ ENGLAND

Court of King Louis XV ~ FRANCE

Court of King Ferdinand ~ NAPLES

and queens and one empress and one pope.

Court of Maximilian III ~ Bavaria

Court of Empress Maria Theresa ~ Austria

Pope Clement XIV ~ The Vatican

He played blindfolded.

He played with covered keys.

He played backward.

He played standing on the furniture.

But Mozart did not play
with the other children,

because his father
made him practice
all the time.

Practice, Mozart,

practice!

Play,

Mozart,

"Wolfgang, are you playing?"

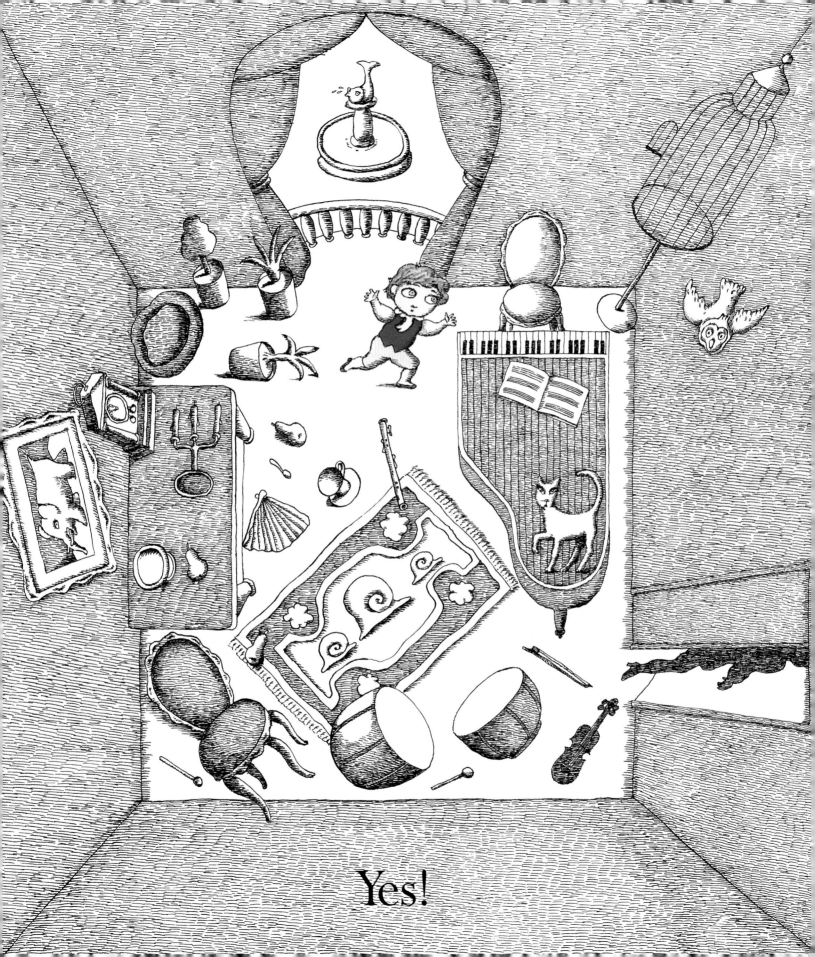

Yes!

Mozart played day and night.

He played in his imagination.

He played in his dreams.

He played for his entire life.

Wolfgang Amadeus Mozart

lived a long time ago,
and he gave us beautiful music.

The whole world
is listening still.
Bravo!

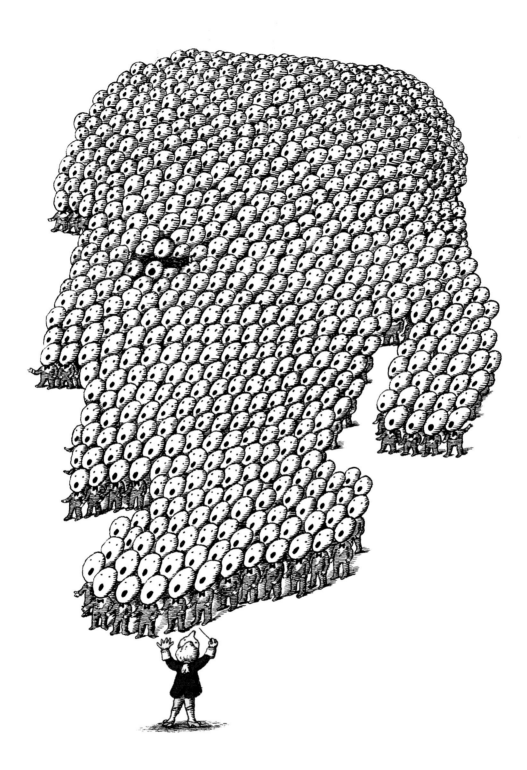

Wolfgang Amadeus Mozart

Wolfgang Amadeus Mozart was born in Salzburg, Austria, on January 27, 1756. His father was a well-respected musician who helped lead the local orchestra. Wolfgang never attended school. Instead, his father taught him and his older sister, Maria Anna (called Nannerl), music at home. Wolfgang learned his first musical piece in only half an hour three days before his fifth birthday, and he wrote his own first composition that same year. By the time he turned six, he could play the harpsichord, violin, and organ. Wolfgang even made sure he and Nannerl had music when they were playing—whenever they took toys from one room to another, one of them carried the toys and the other played a march on the violin. Because he and his sister were so talented, their father decided to take them on tour throughout Europe. The first trip began in 1762, when Wolfgang was just six years old. They toured Austria, Germany, France, England, and the Netherlands, playing for each local court and in private concerts. They usually played two programs a day, with each program lasting two to three hours. People called Wolfgang and Nannerl "child prodigies" or "miracle children." The Mozart family was often on tour during Wolfgang's childhood, and he spent much time in horse-drawn coaches traveling from city to city. While on the road, Wolfgang entertained himself by creating an imaginary kingdom called Back, which he ruled as its king. He also used traveling time and free time to compose. As the years passed, Wolfgang continued to compose many different pieces of music—more than six hundred in all—in many different genres. His last opera was *The Magic Flute,* the story of Prince Tamino, who rescues Pamina, the daughter of the Queen of the Night, with the help of a magic flute. Tamino and his companion, the birdcatcher Papageno, go through tests of their honesty and bravery to discover the truth and free the princess. Mozart died in Vienna, Austria, on December 5, 1791. He is considered one of the greatest composers in the world.